Lucy Flufferbutt

Not Lucy

Lucy

Story by Kalikolehua Orian ♥ Illustrated by Cameron K. Crane

Leaning Rock Press
Gales Ferry, CT

Leaning Rock Press
Gales Ferry, CT 06335
leaningrockpress@gmail.com
www.leaningrockpress.com

978-1-960596-12-3, Hardcover
978-1-960596-13-0, Softcover

Library of Congress Control Number: 2023916663

Publisher's Cataloging-in-Publication Data
(Prepared by Cassidy Cataloguing's PCIP Service)

Names:	Orian, Kalikolehua, author. | Crane, Cameron K., 1994- author.
Title:	Lucy Flufferbutt / story by Kalikolehua Orian ; illustrated by Cameron K. Crane.
Description:	Gales Ferry, CT : Leaning Rock Press, [2023] | Interest age level: 003-010. | Summary: Lucy Flufferbutt is a little hen on a farm. It's cleaning day, and the farmer shows up to clean Lucy's coop, however, Lucy just wants to stay snuggled up in her coop and left alone. Lucy is so annoyed that she ends up creating havoc with the other farm animals. She's afraid that now the other animals won't love her anymore, but as Lucy returns home, she is embraced by her farm family. Everyone can have a bad day, and even though our grumpy mood might affect our friends, true friends will still love you.-- Publisher.
Identifiers:	ISBN: 978-1-960596-12-3 (hardcover) | 978-1-960596-13-0 (softcover) | LCCN: 2023916663
Subjects:	LCSH: Chickens--Juvenile fiction. | Farm life--Juvenile fiction. | Domestic animals--Juvenile fiction. | Friendship--Juvenile fiction. | Animal sounds--Juvenile fiction. | Emotions--Juvenile fiction. | Patience--Juvenile fiction. | CYAC: Chickens--Fiction. | Farm life--Fiction. | Domestic animals--Fiction. | Friendship--Fiction. | Animal sounds--Fiction. | Emotions--Fiction. | Patience--Fiction. | BISAC: JUVENILE FICTION / Animals / Farm Animals. | JUVENILE FICTION / Social Themes / Friendship. | JUVENILE FICTION / Lifestyles / Farm & Ranch Life.
Classification:	LCC: PZ7.1.O718 Lu 2023 | DDC: [E]--dc23

Printed in the United States of America

For Omma,
whose love of books
gave us wings.

For Joni, Esme, and Ann,
who always said we could.

For our family, Peter, Sarah & Matt,
Our puppies Toaster, Laila,
Plum, The Waffle Bandit
Ollie and Gidget.

For Keith, Kyle & Shena, Kip, Kanoe,
and their families.
And, of course,
Alex B.

With Faith and Family
All things are Possible.

"Ohhh, Luuucccyyy,
Lucy Flufferbutt!
It's time to clean your coop."

"I'm here, you see
with everything,

my pail,
and rake
and scoop."

"Brrraaack!"

complained Ms. Lucy,
"I just want to stay!"

"Scadaddle,"
said the
farmer.
"Go out, now,
and play!"

3

So out Ms. Lucy waddled
as grumpy as could be,

looking for a place
to pout until her
coop was all
cleaned
out.

Her feathers so a-ruffle
as she headed towards the house
that she smacked into the Kitty Cat
trying to catch a mouse.

"Meeeow!"
said the cat.
The mouse
said, "Squeak!"
"Bwaawck,"
said Ms. Lucy.
Then
they all
began to shriek!

"What a ruckus! What a roar!
I can't take it anymore."

Then pit, pat, just like that

There goes Lucy Flufferbutt
right back to her chicken hut.

"Shoo!" said the farmer
when she saw
the little hen

"I'll call you
when it's ready
and you can come back in."

So...
back out
went Ms. Lucy
even grumpier than before
paying no attention to
the animals outdoors.
When...

Bump! went Ms. Lucy
as she ran into the dog.
"Hooowwww!!!" cried the dog,
who stepped onto a frog.

"Ribbit," said the frog,
who hopped into the air
and landed on the kitty cat
who didn't like him there.

"Freeee... " squeaked the mouse and scurried towards the house.

mouse.

who let go
of the

the cat,
screeched

"Rawwa!"

"Braaack!"
said Ms. Lucy
as she ran back
to her coop.

"The Farm
has gone doolally;
I'm much safer
on my stoop!"

"Lucy, Lucy Flufferbutt!"
the farmer said again.
"Until your coop is nice and clean
you cannot come back in!"

"Out!" said
the farmer.
"Out this very
minute!"

"I cannot clean your coop
if you insist on being in it!"

"Braaack,"
clucked Ms. Lucy
and ran into the yard.
Again, not watching
where she went

and not

getting

very far.

When...

SPLISH,

SPLASH

What was that?

Icky, muddy Piglets bath!

"Grunt," said the Mama Pig.

"Oink," squeeled the babies.

"Aaaaroowwlll!" laughed the silly dog who fell into the daisies.

Ribbit

Ribbit

Ribbit

Ribbit

Meooowww

Squeek

Swish

Brraack

Hoooowwww

Rawwa!

Breeee

Mmmmmmmlll

Brraack

"Lucy, Lucy Flufferbutt," she heard the farmer call.

"Awwww," moaned Lucy Flufferbutt.

"This isn't fun at all."

22

Ms. Lucy, Lucy Flufferbutt
plopped onto the ground.
Her fluffy, foofy, feathers
all a-ruffle, all around.
She thought about

her morning

with all

the trouble

and kerfuffle

and couldn't believe

the day she'd had

with all the

little scuffles.

Worse, right now the little hen
sat alone, without a friend.

"I've turned the farm
all upside down.
Now everyone
is wearing frowns.

I smashed into
the kitty cat and
scared the mouse,
that's a fact."

24

"I ran into the silly dog
who stepped onto the tiny frog,

then bumped into the mama pig
with all her little babies.
I know my friends are angry

and maybe...

maybe...

maybe...

they don't love
"
me anymore.

"Luuuuucy,
Lucy Flufferbutt,"
the Farmer called again.

"Your coop is clean
and nice and neat.
It's time to come back in."

"Lucy, Lucy Flufferbutt,"
she heard the Farmer call.

And then...

"Lucy!" mewed the cat.

"Lucy!" barked the dog.

"Lucy!" squeaked the mouse.

"Lucy!" croaked the frog.

"Come play!" said piglet babies.

Mama said, "Come home."

"We love you, Lucy Flufferbutt.

You are not alone!"

"Luuucccyyy, Lucy Flufferbut," she heard the farmer, ...and the cat, ...and the dog, ...and the mouse,

...and the frog, ...and the babies,

And the Mama...

ALL call!

29

And Lucy made it home
in barely any time at all.

"Done," said the farmer.
"Cluck," said the hen.
Glad that chore
is over!

Ribbit.

Ribbit.

End.

Author

Kalikolehua Orian, a native of Hawaii, has always had a passion for writing. She discovered a particular joy in crafting children's books in rhyme, often finding inspiration close to home, including "The Mighty Sarah" for her then 3-year-old daughter and "Cameron The Awesome" for her young son. Kaliko's mother, Sue Ellen, a second-grade school teacher, was her greatest cheerleader.

In 2014, Kaliko rescued a small flock of hens from being euthanized. With no farming experience and 300 new mouths to feed, Kaliko quickly found herself in the egg-laying business. With incredible support from her immediate and extended families, she has built her small enterprise into the Kaliko Farms and Omma's Garden brands, sold in the higher-end grocery chains and farmers markets in the Los Angeles area.

Once immersed in the day-to-day lives of raising chickens, it soon became evident to Kaliko that hens had opinions, and the more she observed, the more the stories unfolded. One particular little white hen, a frizzle bantam she named Lucy, provided endless hours of entertainment for the family, and hence The Lucy Flufferbutt series was born.

Kaliko resides in Southern California with her family, puppies, and chickens.

Illustrator

Cameron K. Crane graduated from the University of Oregon with a degree in Arts and Technology. He started drawing doodles almost as soon as he could hold a pencil in his hand, making it an easy choice to pursue a career that included illustration. Cameron has a love for cartoons, Anime, comics, literature and videogames—all of which have contributed to his style of drawing.

Cameron divides his time between his artistic pursuits and helping manage the family farm where he first encountered Lucy Flufferbutt and Friends.

Printed in the USA
CPSIA information can be obtained
at www.ICGtesting.com
LVHW061658221123
764421LV00014BA/1102